A Crack in the
Mirror

stories of other worlds

A Crack in the Mirror

stories of other worlds

WONDERS WILL NEVER CEASE

by Jenny Alexander

Sarah watched her brothers go chasing down the road, kicking an empty beer-can to each other. She hated having to walk to school with them. The problem was, they didn't seem to be capable of walking normally at all. They were always racing on ahead, playing football with bits of rubbish, or else they were dawdling along behind, discussing league tables and championships. And either way, they always managed to end up fighting.

The beer-can went under Mrs Bastable's hedge, and the boys stopped to search for it. By the time Sarah caught up with them, she found them gazing down at a large white object that seemed to be wedged among the bushes.

5

"What do you think it is?" Ben asked, scratching his head.

"It's an egg," said Jamie. He was only seven, but he always had an answer for everything.

"Don't be stupid," Ben retorted. "What sort of bird lays an egg as big as a dustbin?"

"I'm not stupid. You are! Did I say it was a bird's egg? Haven't you ever heard of a dinosaur's egg?"

"Oh, shut up, you two!" Sarah said, irritably. She looked at her watch. "It's five to nine, and we're going to be late. So just leave it alone!"

Jamie said, "If it's an egg, we can crack it open and see what's inside. Right?"

"Right!" agreed Ben.

Sarah was beginning to get angry.

"Leave it alone, I said!" she snapped. "You shouldn't mess around with it anyway. We don't know what it is. It might be dangerous."

Of course, she was quite right. Ben knew she was right. But he hated being bossed around by his big sister. The minute she told him not to do something, he just had to do it. He stepped forward, and gave the egg a gentle kick. Immediately there was a hissing sound, like air escaping through a tiny hole, although they couldn't see any hole in the strange white egg. The children looked at each other. Ben bit his lip.

On the top of the egg, a small blob of pale blue jelly suddenly appeared. Nervously, they all took a step back. Then, like popcorn exploding into one shape from another, the blob of blue burst open and there appeared the strangest creature they had ever set eyes on. It was about the same height as Jamie. The skin of its face was a pale, silvery blue, slick and shiny like the skin of a snake. No mouth. No nose. Just one single eye, which was dazzling blue. It had two arms like a human being, but no feet at all, and its body faded away into a tail of vapour, like a genie or a ghost. The creature was like nothing they had ever seen before; it could not belong to this world. Could it possibly be an alien, a thing from space? Sarah, Ben and Jamie stared at it in astonishment. The creature stared back.

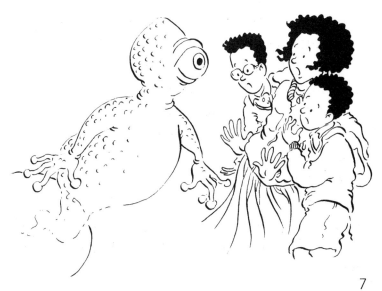

The egg made the hissing noise again and another blue blob appeared. In the blink of an eye, a second alien hovered beside the first. Then, the hissing noise came again. Sarah was terribly frightened, but she tried to stay calm.

"They're not armed," she told herself, as she felt for Jamie's hand, and gripped it tight.

"They're not very big," she told herself, as she tugged at Ben's arm.

"We're sorry if we disturbed you..." Sarah muttered, trying to sound as if she thought it was quite normal to meet an alien on the way to school. She backed away slowly from the egg and its strange inhabitants, pulling her brothers with her.

Then one of the aliens raised his hand and reached out towards Jamie, as if he was going to touch him. Sarah tried to pull Jamie away. But all of a sudden, her brother vanished. Sarah gasped. She looked at her empty hand. She looked behind her, and all around.

"Where's Jamie?" she demanded. "What have you done to him?"

The aliens didn't answer. How could they? They had no mouths. They made no sound at all. One of them pointed his finger at Ben.

"No!" cried Sarah, in horror.

But it was too late. Like Jamie, he simply disappeared.

"Where are they? What have you done with them?" Sarah demanded.

But the words were barely out when one of the aliens turned to point at her as well.

Sarah was relieved to see Ben and Jamie. They were sitting next to her in a round, white room. On a white table in front of them, three glasses were laid out, all filled to the brim with some strawberry-red drink. With a hiss of air escaping, and a sudden explosion into being, the three strange creatures appeared. They gestured to the children to take a glass. The children were too frightened to refuse.

"We shouldn't drink this," Sarah whispered to Ben. "It's like taking sweets from strangers."

"It isn't sweets," he said, automatically contradicting her. "It's just a drink."

"Well, don't drink it," Sarah warned him.

So, of course, he had to do it.

But nothing awful happened to him. He wiped his mouth, and grinned.

"Lovely!" he declared. He was looking at the aliens. "We're going to enjoy being on Earth Pod Zero Four."

Sarah blinked at Ben in astonishment.

"Earth Pod Zero Four...?" she began.

As Sarah looked on in horror, Jamie took a sip of his drink. He drained the glass.

"Mmmm..."

He turned to the aliens.

"Thank you," he said. "The food on Earth Pod Zero Four is very good."

What had happened to Ben and Jamie, that they had suddenly lost their fear, and become calm and happy? It had to be something in the drink. Some sort of drug, perhaps. And where had the term "Earth Pod Zero Four" come from? It must have been communicated to them by the aliens. But how? Through eye contact. That was the only way. The aliens were gesturing to Sarah to have her drink from the remaining glass.

As Sarah raised the glass to her lips, the aliens exchanged a glance and, in that moment, she tipped the drink into her pocket. She couldn't think of any other way of getting rid of it. But the red liquid felt neither warm nor cold nor wet in her pocket, and it had no weight at all. The drink seemed to dissolve into air as she poured it. Gathering all her courage, she looked straight into those alarming blue eyes, and said, "Earth Pod Zero Four is a wonderful place to be."

The aliens began to quiver and fade. For a moment they were like three blue sea-anemones on the smooth white floor, and then, with a sucking noise, they disappeared into it and were gone.

Ben and Jamie lay back on the white benches, and closed their eyes, stretched out like sun-bathers on an exotic shore. Sarah frowned. She had to get them out of there somehow, but it would be difficult if the boys were perfectly content to stay.

Earth Pod Zero Four. Could it be that they were now all inside the white egg underneath Mrs Bastable's hedge? Sarah glanced at her watch. It was still five to nine. She tapped it. How was that possible? How could so much time seem to have passed in a few seconds, and how could so much space fit inside an egg the size of a dustbin?

"We've got to get out of here," Sarah told Ben, softly.

"What's the hurry?" he asked. "It's not as if we're prisoners. Look! There isn't even a door."

He was right. There was an opening on one side of the room, with what looked like a corridor beyond.

"Let's explore then," Sarah suggested, "since we're planning to stay for a while."

"We can't do that," Jamie piped up. Sarah had thought he was asleep.

"Yes we can," she said, and gripping their hands, she dragged her brothers outside.

Her heart was pounding. There was no sound to be heard anywhere. Sarah was terrified that she might suddenly find herself face to face with an alien, as they could appear out of the air at any moment. The first room they came to was identical to their own, but filled with snails and spiders and other creepy-crawlies which swarmed across the floor and walls. None of them spilled over into the corridor. They seemed to be held inside their chamber, as if by an invisible barrier.

"What a beautiful room!" Jamie exclaimed. Jamie, who would run a mile if he saw a spider in the bath! Grimly, Sarah led them on.

In the next room, there were several cats and dogs. In the one after that, flowers and bushes. A room full of rats and mice. A room full of birds. As they explored, Sarah realized what kind of vessel this was. It reminded her of her school project about Charles Darwin, and his travels to the New World. They were specimens. All these birds and plants, these animals – they were specimens of life on Earth. They were being gathered up, to be taken... where? To some other planet? To a space station among the stars? And Sarah, Ben and Jamie were being taken too. What was to become of them all? Sarah shuddered and urged her brothers on.

Now, far ahead, she could see some stairs. White stairs. She glanced behind. No sign of the aliens. How many of them were there? Perhaps there were just the three they had seen. Perhaps they were out gathering more specimens.

But as they neared the staircase, the corridor widened out into a big room, with screens along one side and banks of buttons and dials. The three aliens were over in the far corner, looking at a screen. Sarah pulled Ben and Jamie back into the corridor and put her finger to her lips.

"Let's play a game with them," she said, in a whisper. "Grandmother's footsteps – it'll be fun! We'll try to get past them now, then they can have a turn."

"Where's home?" Jamie asked, and his voice sounded horribly loud.

"The top of the stairs."

"That's too far!" said Ben.

Sarah hoped with all her heart that he was wrong.

"When I say go..." she told them. "Go!"

The three children dashed out across the control room of Earth Pod Zero Four, and up on to the white staircase. They took the stairs two at a time. What was at the top, Sarah wondered? Out of the corner of her eye, she saw one of the aliens turning round...

There was nothing at the top! Nothing but a blank, white wall. Ben crashed into it, with Jamie hard on his heels. And Sarah, too, crashed into the wall. Into it, and through it. With a breath-taking whoosh, they all burst through the blank, white wall and stood on the pavement, dazed and bewildered.

* * *

Whatever Sarah had been thinking about, as she struggled to keep up with the boys, she couldn't remember it now. She found her brothers gazing down at a large white object that seemed to be wedged among the bushes.

"What do you suppose it is?" Ben asked, scratching his head.

"It's an egg," said Jamie.

Sarah glanced at her watch. It was five to nine.

"Leave it alone," she said, "We're going to be late."

Ben grinned. The words "leave it alone" were like a red rag to a bull to him. He moved forward to give it a kick. But for some reason, he changed his mind.

"You know..." he said. "Maybe you're right."

Sarah's mouth fell open.

"Well!" she exclaimed, as they all set off again, together. "Wonders will never cease!"

HAPPY BIRTHDAY, CYBERNIK!

by Jane Irons

April 1st, 2121

There was something odd about today right from the start. To begin with, IMP (that's my Individual Minder Programmer) flashed this weird message up on the screen.

"Happy Birthday, Cybernik!" Well, I know my name is Cybernik, but I wasn't too sure what the rest of it meant. Then I remembered something about birthdays in our learning schedule: people used to celebrate the fact that they were one year older. But that was ages ago, and certainly not on this planet. We don't need things like that in the Fifth Dimension. After all, what's the point of birthdays when nobody grows old any more?

So I clicked the error box. Next I got this message:

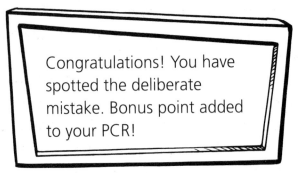

Congratulations! You have spotted the deliberate mistake. Bonus point added to your PCR!

PCR stands for my "personal credit rating". Sometimes I think IMP might have a sense of humour after all.

After this it was business as usual. IMP put up my programme for the day: tablet schedule, learning schedule, activity schedule, leisure schedule and so on. I didn't bother to look at the details: it's nearly always the same, and they soon tell you if you get it wrong.

I was dawdling over my first three vitality tablets of the day when another message flashed up on the screen:

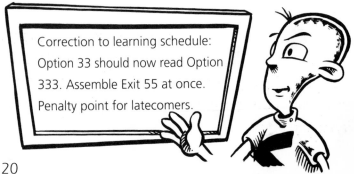

Correction to learning schedule: Option 33 should now read Option 333. Assemble Exit 55 at once. Penalty point for latecomers.

Just my luck, I thought. That means one of those boring educational trips into outer space. They always go on for ever and I'm bound to miss my leisure schedule – again.

I've also been around in the Fifth Dimension long enough to know that "option" means you don't have any choice in the matter. So it was a quick goodbye to IMP, and a speedy sprint along the travelator to Exit 55.

EXIT 55

A group of other people had just got there too. They all seemed to be about my size and shape, but as we don't bother much with interpersonal relationships in the Fifth Dimension I just sort of ignored them.

However, there was one guy who was bigger than the rest and wearing a different sort of outfit. I couldn't ignore him because he plugged straight into my communication system and started jabbering away.

Greetings to all you fellow inhabitants of the Fifth Dimension. I am your Senior Initiative Regulator – "Sir" for short – and I'm to be your guide on Option 333. We have a very interesting Learning Experience lined up for you today – a trip to Theme Park Earth. Now as you all know from your fact sheet, this little planet has just one claim to fame. It happens to be where our Great Pioneers came from long ago. Of course, once they'd discovered the Fifth Dimension they didn't have too much use for Earth any more. But it was decided to preserve the whole planet and turn it into one giant theme park.

On and on he went, droning on about this far-away little planet and the strange lifestyle of its inhabitants. I could see that some members of our group were getting pretty bored with all this, and one or two started fiddling with the controls on their communication systems, trying to turn him off. I was tempted to do the same, but then, to my surprise, I found I was getting quite interested in what Sir was saying.

It seems the inhabitants of this Earth place are all mad about food. First they produce it, then they market it, then they buy it, then they actually *eat* the stuff. What a waste of time and energy when all you've got to do is swallow a few vitality tablets!

I was going to ask Sir some questions about this, but he was already into the last minute-instructions:

To get the full benefit of this Learning Experience, I should make it clear that we will be going back in time. In fact, right back to the 1990s when our very own Great Pioneers were still living on Earth! Of course, Earth is strictly Third Dimension territory. Sounds old-fashioned to you lot, I know, but that's the way it was in those days. So for those of you who haven't made a time-trip before, let me introduce you to your one vital piece of equipment: the DCB, or Dimension Control Box. This ensures we can see without being seen and it also controls the potentially damaging effects of the Third Dimension on our finely-tuned systems. You will each receive your DCB as you pass through the exit. And just make sure that nothing happens to it, or you could find you're spending a little longer on Earth than you intended.

Was this meant to be a joke? (If so, it was the second one that day, and that's way above the national average.) But I didn't have time to wonder about this, as the next moment Sir was clipping the DCB to my wrist.

Hey, this one rattles! Is it meant to do that?

I don't think he heard what I said.

They say too much time travel can do bizarre things to your brain cells. Mine were certainly feeling a little strange by the time we touched down.

Sir's brain cells, however, were obviously just as snappy as ever.

Come on now, you guys, look sharp! This is a Learning Experience, right? Not a Leisure Experience as some of you seem to think. So get moving!

The next moment the escape hatch swung open and we were being shot out on to a curious green surface that felt unpleasantly damp and mushy underfoot.

At once the communication network was jammed with protest.

Ugh!
Sir, do we have to actually walk on this?

It's disgusting!

Sir, I want to go back home!

Now that's quite enough of that! This stuff's called "grass" and it's perfectly harmless, so stop complaining!

I didn't mind crossing the green stuff that much. In fact, in no time at all we found ourselves walking on something smooth and hard, pretty similar to what we have back home. Only this one was really dirty and littered with all sorts of odd things which I didn't recognize. Sir told us the names of some of them:

popcorn packet

sweet paper

drinks can

– all further evidence, apparently, of the inhabitants' obsession with food.

Sir also told us we were in a small town in the west of the planet.

Not just any small town, but the very town where one of our Great Pioneers was born. And we are fortunate enough to be able to visit the actual house where he lives – the house, what is more, where this Great Pioneer is said to have first made contact with an alien!

It was odd walking along the street past weird grey buildings, with primitive-looking transport machines grinding slowly along in the roadway making the most awful noise. But what I found strangest of all were the people. Of course, they couldn't see us because of our DCBs, but we could stare at them just as much as we liked.

They came in all shapes and sizes and colours: old and young, fat and thin, big and small. And the clothes they wore were equally weird, all different colours and styles and textures. Another thing I noticed was that quite a lot of them were eating, even in the street: sucking things on sticks or crunching little crackly things out of packets.

I was just about to ask the names of some of these when I noticed something rather disconcerting:

the people I was staring at were also staring at *me* and giving me some most peculiar looks. What was more, I felt a strange tickling in my nose which seemed to produce an odd rumbling in my stomach.

I tapped anxiously into the emergency helpline, but the line had gone dead. For it was at this moment that we arrived at the house of the Great Pioneer, and Sir had switched off the communication system so that we could all observe one minute's respectful silence.

I'm not quite sure how long a minute is meant to last, but this one seemed to go on for ever. And what made it worse was that, as we were standing there, some unpleasant colourless liquid suddenly started to pour down on us. So when Sir did finally switch on the communication system again, we all started to protest at once.

"Sir, what *is* this? Where's it coming from? Sir, we don't like this!"

You are very lucky to experience it at all! It's known as "weather", and it's the other thing that people here are obsessed with, besides food. And if I get any more complaints, it'll be penalty points all round.

With that Sir hustled us up the steps and into the house, where he assured us we would finally set eyes on the Great Pioneer.

I don't quite know what I'd imagined a Great Pioneer to be like, but what I saw was someone about the same size and shape as me. He was sitting with some other people (called "a family") at a table piled high with food. Sir told us the names of some of the different items.

"Iced buns", "cheese straws", "chocolate biscuits", "birthday cake".

I said the words over and over to myself. The sound of the words was wonderful and the delicious smells of the food were making me feel quite faint.

We watched, fascinated, as the family took bits of the food, put them in their mouths and chewed them up. This went on for some time, and then somebody said, "Isn't it time he cut the cake and made a wish?"

The Great Pioneer stood up and, closing his eyes, whispered (so softly that I could only just hear), "I want to make a really great discovery!"

The next moment he opened his eyes and stared straight at me!

Look!

he said excitedly,

An alien! Over there by the washing machine!

At which the whole family turned round and stared.

I tapped in an urgent message.

Sir, help! I don't think my DCB box is working at all!

But there was no response. Anyway, where *was* Sir? For, looking round to where he and the group had been, I could only see a faint outline and now even this was disappearing fast. In fact, all I could make out was a look of extreme annoyance on Sir's face.

Hey!

said the one they called Grandad.

You in the fancy-dress outfit, are you going to come over and have a slice of birthday cake with us or not?

It wasn't only birthday cake I had, but just about everything else as well. And just as I had been watching them, they now all sat round and watched me.

He doesn't say very much.

commented Grandad.

Perhaps he's just shy.

said the one they called Mum.

Too busy stuffing his mouth!

observed the Great Pioneer.

Eventually I stopped eating because I couldn't eat any more and my stomach was feeling very odd indeed.

Great food. Thanks a million. Funnily enough, I think it's my birthday too. Only we don't have birthdays where I come from.

Where **do** you come from?

asked the Great Pioneer curiously.

The Fifth Dimension.

Where's that?

Oh, everywhere... And nowhere.

For the more I thought about what had happened, the more confused I felt about the whole thing.

The Great Pioneer, however, seemed to understand it all perfectly.

Clearly he has a brilliant future ahead of him. I'm much less certain about me. Looks like I'm stuck in the 1990s, and I'm *not* sure whether that's good news or not. The food's pretty amazing. But as for the rest, well, that's what I'm going to find out.

KRISTEL DIMOND AND THE TIME PIRATES

by Sam McBratney

Hi. DIMOND'S THE NAME.

Hi. Dimond is the name. Kristel Dimond. I'm a Timecop. I was cruising at sub-light speed some-where between Jupiter and Mars when the call came through from Gusty Monroe.

"Get yourself back here, Dimond, we've got trouble. And when I say *trouble* I mean **trouble**."

You should know that Gusty is my boss, and if that man wasn't born Gusty Trouble Monroe, he should have been.

I turned to Lefty, my metal companion. "Sounds like a case of double-trouble, Lefty."

"Indeed it does, Inspector Dimond." Lefty is a robot and I call him Lefty because he sits on my left.

I said, "Doesn't it bother you, Gusty, that I'm on my way to Pluto for a skiing holiday?"

It didn't bother him. *"You get back here, Dimond!"* He sounded hysterical. "Some joker has just come through a Time Hole with something that means curtains for the human race. *Curtains*, Dimond. For the human *race*."

Well, naturally I turned my shuttle around. I belong to the human race, and I'm quite fond of it. "Full proton-drive, Lefty. We'd better see what's up."

"Shall I cancel our hotel booking on Pluto, Inspector Dimond?"

"I suppose you'd better do that, Lefty," I said.

I'm a Timecop, after all. When the human race is about to go down the plug-hole, it's my job to fix things before the final glug-glug-glug.

I docked my shuttle on the Space Station which orbits the Earth and stepped into the zoomtube. Lefty came too. I use him as a kind of butler. The day before yesterday, for example, I sent him out to Pluto to book our skiing holiday. Lefty doesn't grow old or fat or bald and he doesn't get into a foul temper like crusty old Gusty. He's got great brains and a body that can't go rusty. "You'd make a great catch for a lady robot, Lefty," I sometimes tell him. He skis quite well.

FULL PROTON-DRIVE LEFTY...

On the tube I did some thinking about Time Pirates. They are wild characters who nip into the future, grab some wonderful invention, then bring it back and sell it – *before* it has been invented. This is totally illegal, of course. Ever since Time Holes were discovered it has been against the law to use them. We can't have people jumping backwards and forwards through time like grasshoppers. I mean, if somebody nipped back and gave Harold of Hastings a machine-gun, the famous William might not have been much of a Conqueror. Think about it.

JUST HANG OUT YOUR EARS AND LISTEN!

I went in to see what was panicking old Gusty this time. He looked ready for his pension.

"Good morning, Sir."

"Don't 'good morning' me, Dimond, just hang out your ears and listen. Four hundred years from now some genius will invent a device that controls the weather. This device will be of great benefit to humankind, right? A universal blessing."

"Hooray," I said.

"It's called the Rainmaker. There will be no more hurricanes, Dimond. No more floods or droughts. We will have better crops and a planned environment and the Earth shall be a beautiful garden."

"So what's the problem, Sir?" I enquired politely.

"The problem is, some joker has been through a Time Hole and pinched it. He has it *now*. And believe me, Dimond, the weather forecast on Planet Earth will never be the same again. In six months from now the Sahara Desert could be greener than Ireland.

IT'S A NIGHTMARE!

"Using the Rainmaker this joker could start a heatwave in the middle of winter. He could aim a hurricane at New York! Get the picture, Dimond? It's a nightmare! He could start the next ice age tomorrow!"

Poor old Gusty paused to wipe his brow. I'm a cool customer myself, but even I felt warm at the thought of polar bears in my Aunty Mabel's goldfish pond. I mean, she lives just outside Blackpool.

"Which Time Hole did he go through?" I asked.

"The rat went through Checkpoint Charlie," screeched Gusty, who was taking this personally. "Nobody has ever been through it before!"

There are five Time Holes that we know about, each one connecting the future with the past. Checkpoint Charlie is the trickiest devil of the lot to get through.

"Dimond – we have to find this joker. He has to be stopped!" Gusty thumped the table with a hairy great fist, scattering computer disks everywhere.

It's all very well getting grumpy and thumping tables, but where do you actually start looking for a very small needle in a haystack the size of the Universe?

You start by talking to Zeus. This is our central computer. Zeus is a tetrahexahedron (it helps if you say that slowly) with an IQ of about two million. No human being has beaten him at chess within living memory.

I typed in the names of Blackjack Wilcox, John Silver and Lucinda Montcrieff – three of the all-time-greats among Time Pirates. If anyone had the Rainmaker, it must be one of those three. However, according to Zeus, one was in jail and the other two were missing-presumed-dead. It's a risky business going through a Time Hole – you can only see the blighters as you approach the speed of light. Avoid them like the plague, that's my advice.

I had to think, so I got back in my shuttle. All the great detectives have a way of concentrating – where would Sherlock Holmes have been without his fiddle? Me, I like to streak through the Milky Way at the speed of light, zapping asteroids with laser torpedoes. It's relaxing. I was well on my way to the Crab Nebula when a thought hit me.

"Lefty, let me ask you a question."

"By all means, Inspector Dimond," purred Lefty.

"Suppose I wanted to go through a Time Hole. Could you take me through?"

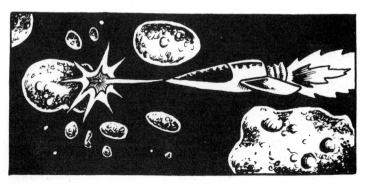

"Which one, Ma'am?"

"Checkpoint Charlie."

"I'm afraid not. The calculations for that particular Time Hole are very complex. Only Zeus could plot a reliable course through it. One mistake and..."

Lefty didn't finish, but I knew what he meant. Make one mistake going into a Time Hole and you pop out the other side like a bit of burnt toast. That's why the pirates end up either very rich or very dead.

I buzzed Gusty on the Visiphone. "Just a thought, Sir. Our joker may be operating from the Space Station."

"Get serious, Dimond. How do you figure that?"

"Well, the way I see it he had to use Zeus to get in and out of the Time Hole. And since Zeus won't give you the time of day unless you enter your personal code – Zeus must know who he is."

HE'S MELTING THE ICE CAPS.

"You mean a lousy *traitor*?" There was a silence. No doubt Gusty was thinking and finding it painful. "Everyone on this station is hand-picked for the job, Dimond. But I'll check that out. And by the way, you might like to know that the beginning of the end has started."

"Explain, please, Sir."

"He's melting the polar ice-caps."

"With the Rainmaker?"

"Exactly. Sea levels will be rising within hours. Do you know what this means, Dimond?"

I sure did. Goodbye Blackpool beach. In fact, it meant Goodbye Blackpool. "I'm on my way," I said.

Two guards met me when I returned to the Space Station. They took my strobe-guns and said, "You're under arrest, Dimond. Get a move on, the Chief wants to see you."

I was dumbstruck, but I went quietly. There had been some sort of mistake. These two gorillas had their wires crossed and Gusty would sort it out.

Things weren't quite that simple. When we arrived at the conference room I saw Gusty, my boss. And *his* boss, the Chief of Police. And *his* boss, the Station Commander.

Gusty glared at me. "I checked with Zeus like you said, Dimond. The day before yesterday someone asked Zeus for the co-ordinates of a Time Hole. Guess who."

I didn't have to guess. The finger of suspicion was only pointing one way. Straight at Yours Truly. I shook my head.

"Are you calling Zeus a liar, Dimond?" roared the Station Commander, who has a face like a purple onion at the best of times. "Zeus can't lie and he can't make mistakes. You used your personal code to plot a course through a Time Hole, and if there's one thing I can't stand it's a crooked cop!"

All the while I was thinking: somebody has used my code to get at Zeus. But who? Nobody knew my code but the people in this room. Down below on Earth the ice was still melting and the water was rising. The world was going down the plug-hole, and they were blaming it all on me. All of a sudden I wished I'd taken that quiet job in the Bank of Mars.

"Gusty, this is ridiculous," I cried out with passion. "I've been framed – maybe by somebody in this very room!"

"That's what I told them, Dimond," nodded Gusty. "You're my best officer. You are incorruptible and I trust you completely."

Sweet, loyal, ugly old Gusty – I could almost have kissed him. But he hadn't finished.

"That's why you have just volunteered to go through Checkpoint Charlie and talk to the folks in the future. Or there won't *be* a future. Unless you happen to be a fish. We need their help to get the Rainmaker back."

Hokey-pokey, hold your horses here! I mean, I'd never actually been through a Time Hole. Those things are dangerous, they scare the pants off me. "Gusty," I said, "can't we talk this over?"

"Either you leave in ten minutes or we stick you in jail," said the Station Commander. I have never been fond of that man.

The Time Hole looked like a round shimmer of light – the entrance to a kaleidoscope hanging in interstellar space. Just staring at it made the butterflies in my stomach feel more like ferrets. I didn't want to go. All of a sudden jail seemed like my idea of paradise. At least I'd live to come out again.

But then I thought: what would I find when I did come out again? There would be no life on Earth as we know it, just the peak of Mount Everest sticking out of an endless sea. It was the duty of Kristel Dimond to go through that Time Hole – my destiny.

I was about to engage full proton-drive when a message came up on my screen.

44

I just had time to fasten my anti-gravity belt and wonder who the *we* referred to, when the kaleidoscope rushed at me and I was going through.

What a trip! Let me assure you that this is one ride they don't have at Disneyland. I was pushed back in my chair so hard I thought I *was* my chair. My blood seemed to boil and set my veins on fire while my poor bewildered heart went crazy. When I dared to look, I saw my craft sinking as slowly as a bubble towards a great city which sparkled like crystals in the middle of a blue ocean.

Ye gods and stars, I thought, I'm in the future! Old Gusty had been dead for three or four hundred years and maybe so had I. Believe me, this is the kind of thinking that gives you goosepimples.

A voice spoke inside my head. *"We understand the problem, Inspector Dimond. We are returning you to your own time with a device to help you find the Rainmaker and destroy it. You must also destroy the device we shall give you. Goodbye."*

Hokey-pokey, we hadn't even said hello! I asked what I thought was a reasonable question. "Don't I get to meet anybody?"

Let's face it, I was curious. Were they the same as us, did human beings still have a chin, were they ten feet tall, what was the latest style – wouldn't *you* be curious?

Perhaps they didn't trust my ancient germs. *"It is not necessary for us to meet."*

"But what happens if I *fail* or something!"

"You will not fail."

And that was that. The voice within my head faded away. The fate of Blackpool, not to mention the entire human race, depended on Yours Truly. Now a little responsibility is fine, but you can have too much of good thing. I can reveal that Kristel Dimond was suffering from a common disease called queasy-knees as she boomeranged back through Checkpoint Charlie.

They had given me a Mindprobe.

All I had to do was point this little thing the size of my fist at people and it read their minds. It told me what they were thinking. Lying was impossible. When I got back, I pointed the Mindprobe at everybody from the Station Commander down to the tea-boy, and you wouldn't believe what goes on inside the heads of some people! I even scanned old Lefty, but all I got was a buzz. His brain runs on batteries, after all.

"Well?" said Gusty. He sounded desperate. Apparently the North Pole was shrinking and an iceberg bigger than the Rock of Gibraltar had sunk an oil-rig near Aberdeen. "Do we have a traitor or don't we?"

"Afraid not," I said. "They're all in the clear. Whoever has the Rainmaker, he's not on the space station, Sir."

"That's it then," wailed Gusty. "Nothing for it now but a hymn and a prayer."

The outlook was bleak indeed. Obviously we were dealing with a madman who was casually wiping out Life on Earth as we know it. Unless you were a fish.

But something was bothering me. Who had access to Zeus? Who knew me well enough to use my code? Who was capable of fooling the Mindprobe? And above all, who didn't give two hoots about the human race or what happened to it? What I needed now were some moments of pure thought. I climbed into my spacecraft and pointed its nose at Ursa Major, otherwise known as the Great Bear.

"Full proton-drive, Lefty. Let's jump some space."

"Certainly, Ma'am."

And then I knew. Call it intuition, call it genius, call it whatever you like. I had what all the great detectives depend on – a moment of clear-seeing. The answer! It felt like a little nugget of pure truth lodged between my eyes.

FULL PROTON DRIVE.

I said, "Lefty, check the airlock for me, there's a good chap."

"Of course, Ma'am," purred Lefty.

Once he was in the airlock, I sealed it. "Lefty – repeat my personal code, please – the one I use for communicating with Zeus."

"By all means. Your code is O5KD661X."

"Thank you. And well done, Lefty.

"My aim is always to please, Ma'am."

"Is it? But it's my guess that you used my code and hopped through time, Lefty. You're the joker we've been looking for all along. And the Rainmaker must be on Pluto, where you went to book our skiing holiday. You may correct me if I'm wrong."

There was a pause. "Your thinking is correct, Ma'am."

"One more question, Lefty. I know how you did it and when you did it. But *why*? That's the part I can't figure out."

BUT WHY?

"It is simply a matter of change, Inspector Dimond. On the Earth there have been single-cell organisms, sea creatures, amphibians, great reptiles, mammals, primates and eventually human life. The next great step in the evolution of life on Earth shall be the development of the independent, electronic, thinking entity."

"The smart machine, eh?"

"Correct. The fittest shall survive, Ma'am. It is my understanding that Humankind is not fit, you grow old and die and you make errors. Therefore the future, and the Universe, is ours. We are at the dawn of a new era. As you say – it is the time of the smart machine."

I pressed EJECT and emptied the contents of the airlock into space, including Lefty. "The Daleks tried it too, my metal friend," I said.

Maybe I should have blasted old Lefty with my lasers, but I didn't have the heart to turn him into space debris. He's out there somewhere between Ursa Major and Orion. Maybe his batteries are still working and he thinks about me the odd time. Goodbye Lefty. And Hello Blackpool.

BEST OF BOTH WORLDS

by Rob Childs

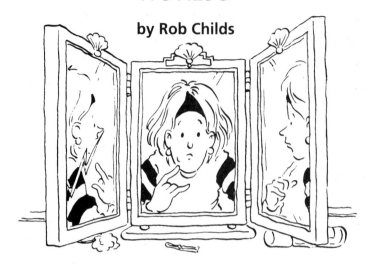

"If only I didn't have this scar!" Becky groaned to the triple reflection of herself in the three-part mirror.

She prodded moodily at the small white mark on her chin and pulled the side panels of the mirror in towards her to inspect it from all possible angles. "I'm scarred for life," she sighed. "Nobody will ever want to go out with me."

The fact that her image was multiplied threefold somehow made things even worse. Becky had already taken out her frustration on the mirror a week ago, lashing out at it with her hairbrush. A wide crack now snaked across the left-hand glass like a crooked smile, as if in mockery of her foolish fit of temper.

"I wish I hadn't done that," she murmured with regret. She didn't really care for having such old-fashioned furniture in her bedroom, but Gran had proudly presented it to her last Christmas. The dark mahogany dressing table and mirror had been passed down through the family right from Gran's own grandmother. As Becky leaned forward to peer more closely at the damage she'd caused, a glint of light from within the crack itself suddenly caught her eye.

It was then that she spotted something even stranger. Her scar had disappeared! Although Becky could still feel it with her fingertip, she could no longer make it out in the broken glass. Puzzled, she straightened up, and her reflection seemed to take just a fraction longer to do the same. She scratched her head and again the matching movement was not quite synchronized. There was only a split-second delay, but the time-lag was enough to jar her brain.

Becky just could not make any sense of it. The only thing it reminded her of was the kind of mirror-image work they were sometimes asked to do in PE, face-to-face with a partner. That usually ended up with both of them dissolving into giggles.

Becky stuck out her tongue and checked round to make sure the other two mirrors were still behaving themselves. The girl in the left-hand glass, too, tried hard to mimic her actions – and failed. Her lips seemed to be trembling, as though in an effort to stop herself from laughing.

Becky's eyes opened wide with amazement. So, too, did those in the mirror, but this time deliberately teasing her. Only this was not some partner messing about, she realized, this was *herself*. The sound of laughter came through the crack in the glass, a bit fuzzy as if recorded at the wrong speed, but she recognized it as hers. Then she heard her own voice too.

"Hi there!"

The greeting was so friendly, it helped to cushion the shock. "Er, hi!" Becky responded after a pause. "Who *are* you? Are you a ghost?"

The girl grinned at her. "Don't be stupid! I'm real, just like you. In fact, I *am* you! Or *was* you – I don't know. I haven't worked it out myself yet."

"I don't get it. What's going on?"

"Search me! A great crack mysteriously appeared in my mirror last week, then it kept going all hazy and I'd get quick glimpses of another person in it. I was nearly scared out of my wits before I saw it was still me – or you, as it turns out!"

Becky shook her head, trying to clear it of some daft dream, but the smiling face in the mirror refused to go away. "So who's the real Becky Johnson, then?" she asked in confusion.

"We both are! Well, sort of, I suppose. Actually, I'm Rebecca now. That's what my friends call me at my new school and I prefer it. I think it sounds more grown up, don't you? I've even got Mum and Dad to use it."

"Hold on! New school? You mean the Comprehensive down the road?"

"No, I never went there. I passed some entrance exams last year to go to the private Grammar school across town instead."

Becky gasped. "Mum and Dad tried to persuade me to do that as well, but I wouldn't. I wanted to stay with Karen and Stacey and that lot who were all going to the Comp."

Rebecca nodded. "I felt the same at first, but I'm glad I gave the Grammar a chance. It's great fun – apart from the homework! And I can still see the old gang when I want to. Best of both worlds, I reckon."

"Both worlds..." Becky mused aloud.

"Sorry, what did you say? You're fading away..."

The left-hand mirror clouded over and when it cleared, Becky found herself staring at a reflection of her own face once more. Mum was also calling her through the door. "Who are you talking to in there, Becky?"

"Er, nobody, Mum."

"Sorry, I thought I could hear voices."

"Oh, yeah, right. Er, I was just talking to myself in the mirror."

The next time Rebecca appeared, two days later, Becky was pulling on a pair of new blue jeans.

"Hey, smart!" came the compliment from the mirror. "I've got some on just like those. Want to see?"

Before Becky could recover from her surprise, a trainer and a denim clad leg suddenly emerged through the cracked glass. Becky squealed in fright and tried to make for the bedroom door. Still only half into the jeans, she tripped over and sprawled in an untidy heap across the carpet.

"Don't panic!" Rebecca hissed as her blonde head popped into view as well, quickly followed by the rest of her body as she jumped from the dressing table to land on the bed. "It's all right. I came through like this yesterday when you weren't here."

"You did what!" Becky gasped, scrambling to her feet and fastening her jeans up. "You can't just go inviting yourself into somebody else's house like that. How long have you been spying on me, anyway?"

Rebecca laughed. "Don't try acting all modest. I'm you, remember, and this isn't somebody else's house. It's mine too."

"How *can* it be? You don't belong here. There aren't supposed to be two of us."

"Yeah, weird, isn't it? There might even be dozens of us around somewhere for all we know!"

"What?" Becky said in disbelief. "All exactly the same as each other?"

"Well, maybe not exactly. I've got nicer curtains in my room than you for a start."

"Huh!" snorted Becky. "Big deal."

"And I don't have that scar on my chin that you get so uptight about."

Becky leapt across to the bed to examine her double. "You lucky thing!" she cried jealously. "How come?"

Rebecca gave a little shrug. "I reckon we must have gone our separate ways before you got it – otherwise I'd have it too. When did it happen?"

"About two years ago. First ride on my new bike and I got knocked down by a car. My own stupid fault. I turned right at a crossroads without looking properly and ended up in hospital."

Rebecca was thoughtful for a few moments. "Hmm, I remember that day as well, going to show the bike off to friends. Dad shouted out..."

"*Be careful. Just go round the block*," Becky finished off for her. "Ah well, I guess you did, and I didn't. If only..."

Rebecca cut her off. "Life's full of 'if onlys'. People are always wondering what might have happened if they'd done something differently."

"Now I know," Becky muttered, fingering her scar again out of habit.

"I don't see why you're so bothered about it," Rebecca chuckled. "It's so tiny you can hardly make it out at all."

Mum's shout inter-rupted them. "C'mon, Becky. Switch the radio off and get downstairs. It's nearly time for school."

Becky panicked. "What are we going to do now?"

"I've got the day off. Think I'll come with you to the Comp and check it out for myself."

"You can't do that. What if somebody sees you?"

"They'll just think I'm you," Rebecca grinned. "So long as they don't see us together. That *would* probably take a bit of explaining!"

"Can't you simply disappear back through the mirror?"

"Charming! Want to get rid of me, do you?"

"No, it's not that, but, well, can you actually get back?"

"Sure. At least, I did yesterday, no trouble. That crack seems to have opened up a link between your life and mine somehow. You just sort of step right through it."

"So I noticed – and you've got better trainers than me, too," Becky sighed. "Ah well, I suppose if I can find you another white top like mine, we might just get away with it. Good job there's no uniform at the Comp."

They both jumped up as the door was pushed open. "Tammy!" cried Becky. "Go away, shoo!"

The spaniel turned its head from one girl to the other in puzzlement and then growled softly at Rebecca. "Well, your dog's no fool," she chuckled. "She spotted the difference straight away. I'm the stranger!"

Becky pushed the dog out of the room. "She won't hurt you. She's just a softie, really. I got her as a puppy when I came out of hospital, to make up for my wrecked bike."

Rebecca waited until Becky left the house before tip-toeing down the stairs herself, hoping to escape unnoticed. "I thought you'd already gone," Mum said from the kitchen as Rebecca opened the front door. "You'll be late if you don't get a move on."

"It's OK, Mum, don't worry," she answered with a laugh. "I'll be there in double-quick time!"

*   *   *

"What's the matter, Becky? You don't seem quite yourself today." The teacher wasn't to know it, but he had never been nearer the truth.

Rebecca blinked. She'd been lost in her own thoughts, miles away from the maths lesson. "Oh, sorry, Sir, just trying to work something out."

The girls around her in class giggled. "What's this *Sir* business?" hissed Karen. "It won't make him give your higher marks, you know."

Rebecca felt herself blushing with embarrassment. She'd forgotten they didn't call male teachers "Sir" at the Comp, the way everyone had to at her own school. Rebecca was getting some very odd looks from her friends and she began to wish that she hadn't let Becky talk her into taking her place in maths – not exactly her favourite subject at the best of times. Lucky Becky was relaxing in the library.

And worse was to follow. While Becky rejoined her group for science, the headmaster caught Rebecca playing the piano in a deserted music room and sent her to wait outside his room. Not knowing where that was, she hid in the toilets and he soon stormed into the science lab demanding to know why Becky was still there doing an experiment.

Fortunately for Becky, the only person not baffled by the mix-up, the teacher insisted she had not left the lab all lesson. The headmaster had to let her off but, even so, he gave the girl a long, hard stare before he stalked back out. "I'm sure it was Becky Johnson at that piano," he muttered.

Rebecca was cornered in the corridor at the start of break by Karen and Stacey. "There's something funny going on with you this morning, Becky," Karen stated. "What is it?"

"Nothing," Rebecca shrugged. "Don't know what you mean."

"Come off it," said Stacey. "Karen saw you slipping in late through the school gates, but I'd been talking to you before registration. Where did you sneak off to?"

"Oh, just nipped down to the shops. Couldn't face another boring Assembly."

"We don't have Assembly today, you know that," Karen corrected her.

Rebecca hesitated. "Er, well, I guess I forgot."

"Like you forgot to tell us when you bought these new trainers as well, I suppose," Stacey accused her.

Rebecca wriggled away. "Sorry, I've got to dash and give some work in. I'll explain later, OK?"

She was just glad they hadn't spotted the missing scar yet as well. "Think I'll leave Becky to sort all that out," she decided. "I'm off home. This is getting too complicated."

Assuming that Mum and Dad would both be out at work as usual, she expected the house to be empty. She was wrong. As Rebecca quietly let herself in with her key, there was a furious barking. She'd forgotten about the dog.

Rebecca flew upstairs, just beating Tammy to the bedroom, and leaned heavily against the door as the spaniel whined and scratched at it. "Huh! 'Just a softie,' Becky said," she panted. "Time for me to go, I reckon."

But it wasn't. It took another two hours of trying before the cracked mirror would finally let her pass back through. But at least it gave Rebecca the chance to make friends with Tammy. Fussing the dog calmed her own sense of alarm, too, at the possibility of being  stranded on the wrong side of the glass. She had discovered that the channel was not always open. It was a matter of waiting for just the right moment.

Taking risks, however, soon became part of the fun and excitement of Rebecca's regular visits. She loved going for walks with Tammy and Becky in the fields, despite having to hide if they spotted someone they knew heading their way. They began to play tricks on their friends, appearing to be in two different places at the same time, and even fooled Gran once when they called on her together.

Gran had just gone to make a pot of tea after letting Becky in through the front door, only to find a grinning Rebecca tapping on the kitchen window. "How on Earth did you get round the back so fast, my girl?" Gran asked in amazement. "Or is it my old legs getting slower?"

It wasn't long before Becky herself plucked up the courage to step through the mirror "to the other side", as they called it, to share Rebecca's world. Becky wasn't too keen on wearing Rebecca's uniform but found the Grammar school much more to her liking than she'd expected – especially once she could recognize all her new friends and remember their names! The best trick they pulled off was when Becky ran the first half of a cross-country course, did a quick switch with her double in the woods and a fresh Rebecca surged on past her friends' tiring legs to finish second!

Then came the most daring transfer yet. After several narrow squeaks when they were almost caught together by parents and friends, Becky and Rebecca decided to swap lives for a whole day, each taking the place of the other completely on their own.

"Just don't say anything else to Dad about beards," Becky warned. "Fancy asking him why he'd gone and shaved his off. He's never even had one here!"

"How was I to know?" Rebecca protested. "Dad on my side grew his beard a year ago. I just presumed yours must have done so too."

"Well he didn't, and now he thinks I was taking the mickey because he keeps talking about growing one and doesn't dare do it."

"OK, I won't mention it," Rebecca promised. "Tomorrow it is, then. We'll try and swap over before breakfast, if the mirror will let us. The school uniform's in the wardrobe, and you've got a maths test!"

Becky groaned. "Now you tell me! On second thoughts, perhaps it might be better if the mirror doesn't work in time!"

Dad came home early the next day. "I may not have grown a beard yet," he grinned at his daughter when she arrived back from school, "but I've done something else that I hope you'll like. Come and see."

She followed him upstairs, Tammy yelping in delight behind them. "Do you think a beard would suit me, by the way?" he asked over his shoulder.

She laughed. "I *know* it will."

Beaming, he threw open the bedroom door. "Surprise! Look, I've bought you a mirror to replace the old cracked one. Perfect match. I couldn't believe it when I saw it in an antique shop in town."

The girl couldn't believe it either. She flopped down in front of it, her head in a spin. "What have you done with the other one?" she cried.

Dad pulled a face. "Don't thank me, will you. No use to anyone in that state, was it? I broke it up and threw it away."

"It's bad luck to break a mirror," was all she could think of to say.

"You're the one who cracked it in the first place, Becky," he laughed. "Bad luck for you, not me."

"Yeah, exactly," she murmured, inspecting her chin carefully in the new glass. "Hmm. I wonder if anyone will actually notice?"

"No," Dad replied, misunderstanding her meaning. "Even Gran won't be able to tell the difference."

She managed a little smile. "Dad," she began, "do you think all of you could start calling me Rebecca from now on, please?"

MOUSE AND THE WITCH-CHILD

by Brian Caswell

Aidan's story *July 7, 1097 AD*

The animal paused in its drinking and raised its head, testing the air. Behind the screen of branches, Aidan watched the deer, and measured the distance, as he reached behind him for one of the arrows that he had stuck into the soft earth.

Carefully, he took aim, and drew back the bow-string. But before he could release the shaft, the rustling noise of footsteps on the far side of the stream sent the animal leaping off into the undergrowth and it was lost from view.

Cursing, he kept the bow primed, and watched the stream bank, waiting for the intruder to appear.

He did not have long to wait.

Parting the bushes where they grew right up to the bank, the young girl put her head through, and looked both ways along the water's edge, before pushing through completely and bending down to drink from the stream.

Aidan held his breath and recited a silent prayer for protection.

Surely, this was a witch-child.

Her hair was long and golden, and hung in unnatural curls around her face.

And her clothing.

It was soft like wool; creasing as she knelt by the water, moving slightly in the late-afternoon breeze. But it was not wool. It shone silver like the metal armour of the knights, who gathered each year for the tournament that Sir Guilliam held to celebrate the victory of the Norman Conqueror.

Who but a witch could weave silver into clothing? Who but a witch would dare wear it? Especially in the lord's forest.

And she had made no effort to be quiet. The deer had sensed her a hundred yards away, and if Sir Guilliam's men were close by, they would be here any moment to investigate.

And yet she knelt calmly to drink.

His fingers tightened on the bow-string, but he prayed that he would have no need to let loose the arrow. What use would a mere arrow be against witchcraft?

He let out the breath he had been holding, and tried to ease the tension in his neck, but he could feel his heart racing, and he knew it was no use.

Then she was staring at him.

Aidan was a skilled poacher. Since the Normans had killed his father, he had kept meat on the table and stocked his mother's secret pantry with animals from Sir Guilliam's woods. He could sneak up on a deer or even a rabbit without the creature sensing he was there. He could hide within a few feet of the lord's men and not be caught.

But this girl, this witch-child, knew exactly where he was hiding. She did not search the bushes with her eyes. She just stared straight at him, as if he were standing in the open.

And her eyes were blue. The deep blue of a summer sky. So blue they almost glowed.

She stood up and faced him, smiling.

Hello. What is your name?

The words came, but her lips did not move. And suddenly he realized. He was not hearing the sound of the words. She spoke them straight into his head.

For the first time, he was truly afraid. He lowered the bow and let it drop from his hands. There was no weapon that could fight magic this strong.

"I am Aidan... But they call me Mouse."

The girl smiled.

Mouse... I like that. I am Rheika. And do not be afraid. I am not a witch. Why do they call you Mouse?

"Because I move so quietly. And I can hide anywhere. Except from you. How did you know where I was?"

It would be too hard to explain. But believe me, it is not magic. I knew; the same way that I know there are men coming. Is there some place you can hide me?

For a moment, Aidan stood confused. How could she know there were men coming? He had the sharpest ears in the village, and he heard nothing.

Then, faintly, he caught the sound of movement in the woods behind her.

"Quick. This way. Cross the stream and come over here but use the stones to get across. Don't wet your feet, or you will leave a trail for them to follow. Sir Guilliam's men are hard to shake if they have your trail."

I fear they have it already.

The girl's words formed in his mind as she made her way across.

Then she was standing next to him. She was smaller than he was and perhaps a couple of years younger. About eleven, he guessed. But she didn't act younger. She stood calmly, waiting for him to speak.

"This way." He whispered the words as he picked up his bow and made his way silently back through the bushes. "And try not to make any noise. They have sharp ears too."

Rheika nodded, and did as she was told.

RHEIKA'S STORY

OK, I know I'm not supposed to make contact with the natives, but this situation was a little out of the ordinary. It was a one in a million accident, but it happened and I was trapped. I needed some help, and he seemed the most likely person to ask.

I told Hanee to have the stabilizers on the capsule checked, but he was probably off somewhere with Ariel and forgot. What he sees in that girl, I don't know.

Anyway, one of the stabilizers must have collapsed because just as I entered the Time-frame the capsule leaned over to one side and rolled down into this sort of gully. I was just lucky that the escape hatch ended up on top when it stopped rolling. Otherwise, I might still be in there.

Nothing was badly damaged, but you can't operate the capsule unless it's standing upright, and the thing was too heavy for me to lift on my own, let alone drag up the side of the hole it was lying in. Like I said, I figured I needed some help.

He was scared of me.

I suppose, when you think about it, he had every right to be. After all, in... what year was it? 1097 AD? I guess I would have looked a bit weird. But he handled it pretty well.

First he got me away from the lord's men. I could see why they called him "Mouse". He moved quickly and hardly made a sound, and he could squeeze through the smallest spaces. It was lucky I'm so small myself, or I might have had trouble following him. We hid in a small cave a few minutes from where I'd hidden the capsule.

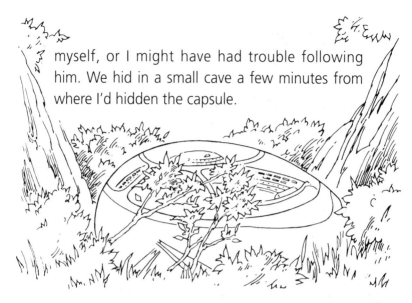

I couldn't hide it as well as I would have liked. I just threw some branches over it, activated the remote force shield and hoped for the best. I was just lucky that where it was lying it was pretty much out of sight already.

I could tell he was scared of me, even without dipping into his thoughts. Back in those times anything you couldn't understand was either magic or witchcraft and I guess nothing about me would have been easy for him to understand. Let's face it, even in the Twentieth Century mind speech would have been pretty frightening so back in the Dark Ages it must have been a lot worse.

I saw him looking at my thermo-suit so I pulled off one of the gloves and handed it to him. He looked at it, smelled it, then slipped it on.

"It's not metal at all," I told him. "It's made of a type of plastic."

That really helped, of course. They wouldn't even invent plastic for another thousand years.

"It makes my hand feel warm." I could see him working things out in his mind. He looked at my suit. "Do you not feel hot wearing that..." He didn't have the words to describe my clothes.

I took the glove back and put it on.

"Where I come from it is much hotter than here. I would feel cold if I did not wear the suit."

I could see he was still confused. "But it is summer," he said. "It does not get any hotter than this."

How do you explain the Greenhouse effect and centuries of global warming to someone who doesn't even know that the Earth is round?

I didn't try.

"I really need your help. Without it I will not be able to get back home."

Home, he understood.

"Where is your home?"

"Far away." I didn't bother trying to give any more details.

What could I say? Sixteen hundred years in the future?

I suppose he accepted the answer, because he just nodded.

"How can I help?"

The million-dollar question.

"How strong are you?" I asked.

Aidan's story

Slowly, they removed the branches that covered the capsule. When it was revealed, Aidan stood back. The machine was roughly egg shaped, but the clear plastic bubble which formed its top half showed the complex controls and information screens.

One of its tripod stabilizer legs had snapped in half, while another had been badly bent when the capsule had rolled down the side of the small gully. Rheika examined the damage again and shook her head. It was hopeless. There was no way that the stabilizers could be repaired in such a primitive place.

She looked at Aidan and tried to smile, but her frustration and her fears overflowed. She began to cry.

If I can't fix it, I won't be able to get home.

Aidan looked down at her. Suddenly, she seemed less powerful. She looked just like his sister, Regan – except for the way her hair curled, and the incredible colour of those eyes.

He reached out and wiped away a tear.
"We will need help," he said.
But...
"We cannot lift it alone. Come, try."

Together, they strained, but the capsule barely moved. Aidan sat down on a rock.

"If we cannot even turn it how can we carry it to the top of the bank?" He looked across at the machine. "What is it?"

There was no way to explain. For a moment, Rheika stood silently, then she drew a breath.

I suppose you could call it magic. Good magic. Where I come from we know many things and we travel to many places and... times. To learn about people and where we come from. But we are always careful never to be seen. Until now. You saw me. No one must know. We cannot ask for help.

"One man." Aidan stood up. "Brendan the Smith. He was my father's friend. He will help and ask no questions."

How can you be sure? As soon as he sees...

"That's the point! He can't see. He went blind three years ago. He can no longer shoe a horse, or fire a forge but he is still the strongest man I know. And he will help me. For my father's sake if not for mine. Stay here with the egg and I will go for him."

And without waiting for her reply, he was gone.

RHEIKA'S STORY

What could I do? I couldn't move the capsule and I couldn't leave it there, so I had to trust him. And I was pretty sure he'd do what he promised.

What amazed me about Aidan was the way he... accepted things. He asked a few questions, but he didn't seem to mind not understanding the answers. I suppose in those days there was so much about the world that no one understood that they had to accept a lot more without too many questions.

It was after dark when they came back. Aidan was leading the biggest man I've ever seen. He was well over two metres tall and looked as strong as an ox.

I told Aidan that I'd been thinking. We didn't need to get the "egg" up to the top of the bank. As long as we could stand it upright, I could make it work and I could get home.

I looked at Brendan's eyes. There was a white film over them and I knew that there was no hope that he would ever see again. Back home, with laser surgery, they could fix him up in half an hour, but here...

I shook my head as I helped Aidan and the big man to lift the capsule.

For a moment, it seemed as if even Brendan's strength would not be enough. Then I felt it move. The soft earth sucked a little as the weight pulled free, but then it was standing upright and Brendan was holding it there until we wedged it with rocks and pieces of wood, so that it would not fall.

I was ready to go.

I looked at the two of them standing there. I owed them so much. But there was nothing I could give them.

Then it struck me. I'd broken so many rules already that one or two more couldn't hurt. I took the locket from around my neck and handed it to Aidan. He looked at it in wonder before closing his hand on it.

Then I spoke to Brendan. Not in mind-speech but in words.

"You have helped me. If you will trust me, perhaps I can help you."

As I spoke, I looked at Aidan. He placed a hand on the big man's shoulder and squeezed. Brendan nodded without saying a word.

"Wait here," I said to Aidan. Then I led Brendan into the capsule and strapped him into the passenger seat.

Aidan's story

The moon was full, and its light shone on the capsule as Rheika closed the hatch. Inside, Aidan could see the two figures. His father's friend and the strange girl.

How did he know she was to be trusted? He just knew.

Inside the capsule, she leaned forward and pressed a button. For a moment there was nothing but a slight droning sound. Then the capsule simply disappeared.

Barely a heartbeat later, it was back, a few yards further down the gully, and standing firmly on three spidery legs. The hatch flew open, and Brendan jumped out.

"Aidan, boy! I can see. I don't know where she took me, but they fixed my eyes. I can see better than ever. It's magic boy, that's what it is."

Good magic.

Aidan remembered the girl's words.

Rheika did not come out of the capsule. Somehow he knew she wouldn't.

I have to go, Aidan. I'm in enough trouble already. Thank you, my friend. Goodbye.

And then the droning started, and the capsule disappeared. This time forever.

He looked down at the locket she had given him. There was a button on the side. He pushed it, and the two halves sprang open.

Inside, was a picture of the girl – the golden hair, the incredible blue eyes. And as he looked at it, the picture smiled.

Quickly, he snapped it closed.

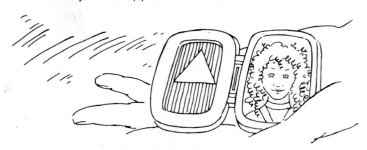

"What's that, then?" Brendan moved up beside him. Slowly, he opened his hand.

"Fairy gold. Isn't it amazing what you find out in the woods?"

"It is, lad." The big man smiled and looked up at the moon for the first time in more than three years. "Sometimes you can just be lucky."

Together, they turned and headed back through the woods towards the village.